A DREAMER'S QUILL

COLLECTION OF SHORT STORIES

RIDDHIRAJ

Made with ♥ on the Notion Press Platform
www.notionpress.com

To My Lil Boss <3

Contents

Preface

This book is a collection of short stories venturing into different genres. I have been told that I have a knack for writing so I thought to myself, why not put it to the test? As a student, there's not much time between a six hour school schedule and entrance coaching. But, somehow I managed to put my views on paper and present it to you guys. I wrote this book as a platform for furthering and making the people aware about my writing and also to address the dwindling reading habits of teenagers nowadays. I thought that maybe if they see someone else of their age group writing a book and getting it published, they might start reading too and maybe at some point in their life, it will be their name in the Pulitzer Prize shortlist. I know it's a far fetched goal to be someone's inspiration, but what's a dream without a little touch of impossibility to it. So that's all from my side. Hope you guys like the book and enjoy reading it . Happy reading !

Acknowledgements

I would firstly like to thank my parents, especially my mother who has motivated me and been on my hair since day one to write and publish this book. She's the main reason that this book is getting materialized in the first place. I am also really grateful to my English teachers, who have been with me along the way and helped me with anything and everything that I needed. My friends also have been a big part of this. They have always motivated me to do something big using my writing skills and they have always had my back and admired what I write. Lastly, I owe a great deal of gratitude to all the readers who read, are reading and will be reading my book for providing me with much needed exposure and a quality platform to showcase my skills.

1

COLOURS OF LOVE

Bustling streets, traffic jams, hand carts... just a routine Muzaffarabad day for Shazia as she left her home at 5 in the morning for Mall Road, which was her usual haunt. Shazia, just like many other girls in her slum sold paper napkins and handkerchiefs at traffic crossings. Her father fled soon after her mother got pregnant with her and her mother died giving birth. So, she's been subject to the rugged,vile and cruel Pakistani foster system. But, at present she sells enough napkins to sustain herself at a bare minimum level. It was a usual day at the crossing with the road flooded with public transportation and rickshaws. But in the midst of this ordinary crowd, there was something out of the ordinary. A blue Mercedes C-Class with tinted windows approaches her. The driver lowered the window and the tinted glasses gave way to an extremely handsome gentleman probably in his late 20s. Hurriedly, he bought a napkin for himself and rode away into the dusty street towards the Corporate Sector Road. But the 30 second encounter was enough to fuel Shazia to go home and look him up. But she didn't know his name, how was it possible to look him up? "Driving a Mercedes, going into the

Corporate part of the town, expensive clothing, arrogant looks,hmm.. all this points to a high post in a reputed company. Let me look up young directors on the web, maybe I'll get some info". She searched the web for young directors and it didn't take long for her to find him, a familiar face with a dazzling smile. But, Shazia was not too shabby herself. Her silky brown hair were arranged into fringes over her forehead and her rosy cheeks were accompanied by a sweet smile and dimples. She had a fair complexion and was thin but without the taut look of wiry people. It was as if an error of destiny had forced this child of Allah onto the streets. Next morning, she left for work as usual. The crossing was a busy sight but Shazia for once did not care about the napkins being sold or not. She had her eyes glued on the street for a Blue Mercedes. 7 AM... 8AM...9AM...10AM...11AM...time passed by but there was no sign of him. At last, just as she was leaving that crossing to get food, the C-Class pulled up beside her. "No napkins for me today,ma'am?" Shazia, flustered by the respect she was getting from a person of her age group, replied in a whispering tone "If you'd like some, then please,uhh.. Mr. Rizwan Qureshi." Surprised at being name-called by his not so old acquaintance, he replied "So you looked me up,huh? Splendid, that relieves me off the awkward task of having to introduce myself and I'll take all the packets of napkins you have,uhh... what do you call your pretty self miss? " "Shazia", she said in a quivering voice. "Well, a pretty name for a pretty face. I'll go now 'cause I'm running really late. It was nice meeting you. See you around." As he started the car she hesitatingly screamed out "Bye, nice to meet you too." The rest of the day was a rose coloured lens for her. She had fallen and fallen hard for him. But deep in her heart, she knew the ground reality. She could never be with him. The society just won't allow it even if he wanted to. Lost deep in her thoughts she returns home. That night, her friend Nazma, invited Shazia to her house for dinner. But as dinner was being served, Nazma noticed Shazia lost in her own thoughts and shouted, "Earth to Shazia! You here ?" Shazia smiled and replied, "I am here dumbo, you don't need to shout your lungs out." At the same time, she thought to herself "How can I be here when I'm in my own world.. A world filled with Rizwan and Rizwan alone." A greater determination and enthusiasm now took over her and enhanced her will to work. She would go to the crossing everyday and Rizwan would buy all her napkins and They'd have their little chats which grew by the length everyday. It was the monsoon and being an underdeveloped hilly region, Muzaffarabad was prone to landslides. Such a landslide had claimed Rizwan's parents' life. Both of them were diplomats. They were going to Srinagar around the same time 5 years back for a round table conference, but they never even made it there. They were struck by a landslide on the way and were crushed beneath the rocks. "I didn't even get to say goodbye or see their bodies", he said while describing this whole incident to Shazia over a cup of tea, which was like amrit in the freezing monsoon winds. "Well at least you saw them, I couldn't afford the luxury", said Shazia in a trembling tone. They both just sat there lamenting and remembering their losses with the otherwise romantic but presently gloomy damp weather as a companion. "Well, lunch's over gotta get back to the office, see ya!" He exclaimed as he walked out of the tea stall and went into the car. Shazia waved him goodbye and went on with the other side of the road to her usual haunt. That night he couldn't sleep. He just could not for the sake of him, get her out of his mind. It had been like this for the past few weeks. Since the day he met her at that crossing. "But society won't let me be with her. The Managing Director of Awakened Technologies Limited with a street vendor. The society just won't allow that and my parents? They wouldn't have allowed this either and I don't want to disrespect their memory." His mind ran in all directions, from everywhere to everywhere. "But if I can't be with her then what should I do about the burning desire of just laying my head over her chest to hear her heartbeat resonate with mine, feel her soul unite with mine, to adore her charm as strong as the vine and at that moment, I could stop the world, that's all I wish for." Weeks went by, and the bond between them was never stronger. They had become the best of friends, hanging out regularly and telling each other literally everything. The way both of their eyes sparkled instilled in their respective selves a hint that the other person might just be feeling what they were. "Does she like me too?" "Does he like me too ?" "Nah, that's just too absurd." The next morning it was Friday so they met each other at the usual time at the Dargah for the routine prayers. After the prayers were done, Rizwan told her that it was his birthday tomorrow and added stutteringly, "I..um, I... just wanted to ask if uhh you'll be good with coming to my house tomorrow for a cutting chai and our usual talk along with a little bit of birthday celebration. I hate to admit it but I don't have anyone else to celebrate my 30th birthday with. Perks of having to be an apparently cold MD" "Sure, I'd love that", she replied. Not being able to control his happiness, he said, "Okay then, it's a date". Having realized what he just said, his face turned red and he tried to correct himself by saying "I mean, not a 'date' date , you know I just meant the expression they use in the West." Shazia smiled in the most charming way possible and said "I get it, it's a date."

They both laughed heartily at this and then left for their respective destinations. "675, Ali Jinnah Street , I'm at the right address I guess." Standing before her was a fantastic but intimidating mansion painted all in brown with transparent glass windows and a massive pool beside a colourful garden. She rang the door bell. After a few minutes, the door opened and emerged a familiar face "Asalam Alaiykum, Shazia" "Alaiykum Asalam." They both greeted and hugged each other and went on inside. Amazed by the sheer space Shazia exclaimed "Wow, your kitchen trumps the size of my whole house!" Rizwan just laughed and asked her about her day as a bid to change the topic, and it worked. They talked about many things that evening but his monetary superiority wasn't one of them. "Well, it's getting late now. I should get going." "Well wait, I'll drop you off ", he said while grabbing the keys and opening the door for her. Weeks went by without anything eventful happening apart from the sleepless nights they both were having thinking and fantasizing about a situation where they were together. It was autumn now. The leaves started getting orange-ish and falling off but their bond was stronger than ever. The wind was unbearably cold that morning when Rizwan said "How about we meet up at your place tomorrow evening" "But my place has bearly any space for me to live alone. Won't you feel uncomfortable", she said, praying to God that he finds a reason to come to her house nonetheless. "C'mon now, I've been to humble houses before. I'm not a rich snob, you know. Besides it's not the house that I'm interested in..." Oh how badly he wanted to say that it was her that he was interested in but instead he said, "... It's the hospitality. Moreover, it's the people that make a house into a home. Not the space,right?" "Right", she said "My place it is." As he raced away in his blue Mercedes, she could feel her heart racing as fast as a Formula1 racecar moving towards the finish line. She smiled briefly to herself before engaging in selling napkins for the rest of the day. The next evening he was at her door as promised. She opened the door and welcomed him inside. The house was a really humble one. Although it was a pucca one, the bricks had no paint and the furniture was on the cusp of breaking off. Moreover, the house was located in the midst of a slum. But that didn't prevent them from having the best evening ever, They cooked dinner and ate together , they talked about their respective days and Rizwan explained how he got his drinking habit. Shazia gave him an ultimatum that if he drinks more than twice a month in the future, their friendship is gone. Rizwan said, "Don't worry, being around you makes me feel obligated not to drink. So I guess you make me a better person then?" "Well, good for you", Shazia said in a sarcastic tone and they both started laughing together. The next one and a half month went by without much happening but considerable progress in their friendship. Their bond had become virtually unbreakable. They were having the time of their lives. Drinking chai together, frequenting each other's house and at the same time earning a livelihood. But, the elephant in the room still remained unaddressed. They both still hadn't confessed their love for each other. "If only we could be together", they both said to themselves before falling asleep every night. Finally, it was 14th December. Shazia was turning 28 the next day. While they were drinking their usual morning cutting chai, Rizwan proposed that they should meet up in his office the next day to celebrate her birthday in his cabin. Shazia agreed even though she very well knew she was inviting another sleepless night for herself and indeed she couldn't sleep a wink thanks to the combined excitement of her birthday and a celebration with Rizwan. The next day came soon enough. She went to his office as scheduled at 6 in the evening. Everything was going merrily, they popped open a bottle of champagne, cut the vanilla flavoured cake and had ordered takeout. But suddenly in the midst of the silence there were series of gunshots. “Those are no ordinary guns. These are the gunshots of an AK-47. This means we’re probably... uhh... how do I say this ? uhhh....” “Under a terrorist attack ?”, Shazia continued and Rizwan nodded his head. He unlocked his phone and he got to know that the whole corporate sector was under a terrorist siege and no wonder that terrorists had struck the most significant building in the whole square, the building where Rizwan’s office was located. The sound of gunshots and grenades now became even more frequent. The smell of gun powder and smoke dominated the air. The occasional scream let out by the victims sent chills down their spines. They quietly hid below a table in Rizwan’s cabin. “This floor is too high up . They won’t come here. Don’t worry.”, said Rizwan. “But what if they do ?” Rizwan smiled reassuringly and said “Then I’ll protect you till my dying breath, I promise.” Although the gunshots kept frequenting their ears, no one had yet come to their floor. But for the life of them, they couldn’t dare to step out of their hideout to look outside. The police ground force had already arrived but they couldn’t go into the building as they had orders to just set up a perimeter and wait for the special task force to arrive to avoid loss of personnel. Suddenly there was a blink sound. Somebody had come up to their floor. The presence was confirmed by the sound of the lift opening. “Come quickly , follow me. There’s another elevator on this floor. If we take it and reach the ground floor, we will be safe .” They ran towards the east side of the floor and pressed the button to call the elevator and waited frantically for it to arrive. As it arrived, they stepped into the elevator and let out a sigh of relief. “We'll be safe, don't worry”, assured Rizwan as by this time Shazia had burst into tears and was sobbing. They reached the ground floor, saw the ground force outside the exit gate and made a run for it. They had almost reached the exit when they heard someone shout in Urdu. It was a terrorist. Rizwan stopped to look backwards and saw the terrorist aiming his gun at Shazia and as the terrorist shot out the bullet, Rizwan leapt in front of her and got shot right in the chest. By this time, Shazia was with the ground force. Some personnel, refusing to let a man die in front of their own eyes, went inside and brought out Rizwan's body. But they realized it was too late and that he would not survive the ride to the hospital. So they left the body for Shazia to say her goodbyes. Shazia was shivering . She was totally dumbstruck. She just couldn't believe that this had happened. This initial shock led her to burst into tears. The love of her life wasn't on this mortal plane anymore. In an attempt to hug him, Shazia felt something familiar in his shirt pocket. Inside, She found a napkin that he had bought from her and a paragraph written there for her. “I love you, more than anyone I've ever loved. I wanted to say this to you but I just kept thinking what the society would think about us being together. But, I just can't hold it back anymore. On this 28th Birthday of yours, accept this as a gift from my side .” Suddenly after reading this, The snowfall felt colder much like the lifeless corpse of the dear love laying in her arms. The melanchalous winter landscape and utter chaos gave way to a heart that had been broken into a thousand pieces. A heart which harbored for long an unconfessed love.

2

MINDSCAPES

"Sam! Sam wake up, you're late for school!", shouted his mom as she burst into his room. "Mom, you gotta respect my privacy. I was about to get ready after finishing this round." "Waking up to video games... Just great! Whatever, come down fast or you'll be late for school and I am not gonna drop you off today young man." "What makes you think I even slept last night huh?", said Sam in a matter of fact tone. His dad was a scientist and was presently in Antarctica doing research on the rapidly melting glaciers. This trip of dad had led to Sam treating video games as his wife. His mother was a cardiothoracic surgeon in a reputed hospital in New York. City life was not doing him good. He had no friends, no sense of purpose, no aim in life, no parties, not much time and attention from parents and a fragile will to live. On top of all these were the hormones, which, by the way weren't helping much either. They say teenage are the years when life seems more lively than it actually is but for him it was as dead as ever. The only time he felt a sense of purpose and had a definite aim was when he played video games. The will to win and advance into the next level gave him a strange sense of responsibility and obligation towards his teammates. It also instilled in him a much needed confidence boost as with advancing to the next level came an added bonus of greater confidence of advancing even further. So basically the life skills that he was obtaining at the age of 16 was solely from video games. Talking about a teenager's life, real life I mean, the first thing that comes to mind is homework. Sam was not really sunshine in that area too. He had tons of homework to do but on the other hand, he had every one of the daily quests and missions of the game completed. But, the one thing that was going good for Sam was that he was not bullied at all unlike many other unlucky and poor souls. The children at school have never paid him attention enough to bully him. Blessing in disguise, I guess. But he got attention in the game though. He had one of the highest scores in the survival mode of the game. Even after having an athletic physique with a fair complexion, curled hair, brown eyes, abs and veiny arms accompanied by a 5 feet 10 inch height, he has had no luck in the romance department. His love life had been an absolute nada. But unlike other teenagers, he didn't really care. All he wanted was to become the highest rated player in the history of the game called Real Life Evolution. It was a virtual reality based game which portrayed the current situation in the brain onto the screen as different missions and with hurdles being the different problems being processed by the brain at the time. It was a particularly stressing day for Sam at school that day. He couldn't wait to come home and dive into the simulation. The chemistry teacher had left no stone unturned to make Sam visible in a world where he was way better being invisible. The history teacher told him off for not submitting the assignment even a month after the due date. Every teacher had something to say to Sam today and not in a merry way. Controlling the urge to beat the shit out of his school locker, he came home and wore the VR box as if he was the king and it was his crown. So he started the game. But after a few minutes of play, the game started glitching. Everything in the game started blinking and emitting robot like sounds. After a few seconds, he felt like he was being sucked into a vortex. Screaming his lungs out, he felt his voice reverb around him in all directions as if he was in the bathroom. "Mom!! You there !?" He fell into a dark pit filled knee deep with sewer water. He started walking without a destination. He did not know where he was going. For a while he thought it was all VR, but then he noticed the felt the water ebbing against his calves. It was all real. Somehow he was in this...place. After walking for a while, he noticed a light at the far end of what seemed like a tunnel. A bleak light. But he ran towards in nonetheless. As he started running the whole place started getting lit by torches and he realized that he was inside the very game he used to play. Somehow he had become the very character in the game which involved solving the riddles hidden deep inside his own teenage brain. As easy as it seemed solving the riddles and overcoming the hurdles buried in your own brain, it was a really difficult task. A teenage mind is full of activity and with more activity comes more problems. Suddenly a vibey music started playing and the rusty gates before Sam opened with a creepy creaking sound. The in-game system started announcing all instructions. The voice felt like it was tickling his belly. He listened eagerly to the instructions. But the last one was scary to say the least. "You will not be able to return to the real world lest you should defeat the Boss within the three lives you've been given." A chilling shiver ran over Sam's whole body and The body hair was totally upright as if screaming "Present ma'am" to the teacher during attendance. “Ready,Player1 ?”, roared the system “R-r-r-ready”, he replied nervously while playing scenarios in his head where he might not be able to return to the City at all. “Let the mind games begin!” He started walking towards a vast space with a bad weather. The rain was torrential accompanied by the occasional lightning flash and the deafening sound of thunder. Apparently it was night time in the game. The tasks in the game were to be completed by determining the problem in the brain symbolized by the task and then somehow decipher how to complete the task by overcoming the hurdles. The first task at hand was called “Rescue The Citizen”. In this task, there was a similar version of him tied with a rope and being descended slowly but steadily towards an up and running chainsaw. Guarding this setup were his own classmates. All big, hunky and sturdy as if they were ready to rip Sam off to shreds. Not being able to figure out the symbolism, he decided to dive head first into the crowd. A punch... A kick.... BOOM!.... BAM!.... That is when he remembered that this is not just a VR game anymore, what happens here, happens to him in real life. “Goddamit, the first task has not even started and I'm already all bloodied up”, said Sam wiping the blood pouring down his nose. “Hmm... What could the hidden truth behind this task be ?” He stood there thinking long and hard about the hidden symbolism. That is when he realized that the citizen that needed saving was a younger version of himself. Although he was invisible to the classmates around him, he realized that he himself had been influenced by those very classmates. Dressing style, walking style, hairstyle, attitude etc. etc. In this process he had lost himself, the original Sam Brody. That is why the citizen had to be saved and to be saved , Sam had to fight off his classmates. Now that he had figured out the symbolism, he had to now figure out a way to save the citizen. Hand to hand combat was not an option. He was bitterly outnumbered. Then he remembered that this was a symbolic simulation of his own teenage brain. So, if somehow he convinced himself that he is not influenced by his classmates, he would be able to eliminate them from this equation and finally save the citizen. But the time was running out. With each passing second, the citizen grew closer to the chainsaw. He was trying to convince his brain that his classmates held no power over him, but to no avail. But actions speak louder than words. So he changed his hairstyle, wore his clothes in a different way and resorted to his original walking style. One by one, his classmates started disappearing. At last, only two classmates were left idolizing whom, he had started going to the gym. Given the time constraint and lack of options, Sam had no other choice than to fight them off and so he did and so did he. He emerged the winner and then ran swift as a cheetah towards the chainsaw setup and saved the citizen just on the brink of being converted into shredded meat and with that the first task was complete and he could finally let out a sigh of relief. The next few tasks were overcome by him fairly easily by him through a convincing of the brain through his actions that he was no longer a sorry victim of that problem anymore and so went peer pressure, failed romance, body obsession, mood swings , overthinking, lack of sense of purpose, lack of a definite goal in life and procrastination. Next up was his ADHD. "Phew... what an adrenaline rush. Just three more tasks to go." Blissfully oblivious of his impending doom, he advanced towards the next task. This was going to be particularly tricky for him as ADHD was a disorder from which he was suffering for a long time and it had ingrained itself into his body as if it was a part itself. As he advanced further, the bumpy pathway gave way to the visible task which seemed to be divided into two segments. On one end he could see a cold waterfall with a stone beneath it meant most probably for sitting. On the other end he could see a shooting range. That was the moment he realized that this was the task aimed at curing his brain from ADHD. The waterfall to prevent hyperactivity and the shooting range to enhance attention. Above the waterfall he could see a timer timed at 10 minutes. "What the hell!! I have to sit beneath this freezing cold waterfall for 10 whole minutes? Ain't no way." At the far end of the shooting range he could see a scoreboard. On one side it displayed his points and on the other side the points that needed to be scored "1000 points! To think I've never ever lifted a bow in my life. No pressure." He went to the waterfall first and prepared himself to sit calm in the laps of the freezing cold water for 10 whole minutes. "It's my funeral. God save my soul now." The first 3 minutes went by without much discomfort. Then started the shivering and his hyperactivity also kicked in. He controlled all this for the next 4 minutes. Now his condition was really dire. He was shivering beyond measure. The shivering caused his back to ache and his hyperactivity begged every inch of his body to get up and leave the waterfall . But he knew he had no other option so he held on for the next 3 minutes and the task was finally over. His face was all red. He was shivering beyond measure and his body hair was all up indicating the goosebumps arising from a state of shock. The game provided him a change of clothes which he put on and after a break of 20 minutes, he went on for the next part of the task. As he approached the enclosure from which the arrow had to be struck, he noticed there was no bow or arrow present. But how was he supposed to put down the targets then? "Ugh, I've had it with these riddles. I've solved enough to last me a lifetime." He thought to himself "If this exercise is designed to increase my attention span then it's only natural that focus is involved. So how about I focus on the bullseye and imagine an arrow going straight for the bullseye and keep imagining this till the arrow makes contact. That requires a lot of attention right ?" He implemented this and it actually worked. The short and medium distance targets were fairly easy to hit. But as usual his ADHD made it utterly difficult to focus properly and hit the long distance targets with precision. But, after half an hour of mind wrenching, brain bending concentration, he was able to shoot down all the targets and attained the required score to move forward. The next 2 tasks were Boss Level tasks. Intermediary Boss Level and Final Boss Level. Both these tasks were designed to overcome the prime teenage problem,namely, defiance. In the intermediary level, defiance towards teachers will be dealt with while towards parents will be dealt with in the final level. He advanced towards the intermediary boss level. In front of him stood his school, all empty with a creepy vibe. He went in . An announcement started roaring "Once you come in, there is no going out unless you do everything the teacher says. You will be met with a chore at every gateway. You have to complete it without fail and within the stipulated time to advance to the next level. For assistance, you have Ms. Brown by your side. Complete the tasks with her help and strictly follow her guidelines or stay trapped here forever." A buzzer went off indicating that the time had started. His principal Ms. Brown looked creepy as usual. He had 3 minutes to complete every task. He went through the tasks pretty easily. Defiance towards teachers had never been much of a problem for him. So he passed the intermediary level tres facilement. Up next was the Final Level. Although defiance towards teacher was not much of a problem for him, defiance towards parents was a whole new chapter for him altogether. He was defiant towards parents from the very start. He felt that if he was not getting their deserved time, he owed no duty of care towards them. "This one's going to be a hard one", he said. As he headed towards the next and the final task, his heart was beating rapidly. His legs were aching and his head seemed as if it would fall off his neck. As he reached his final destination, before him stood a really spooky and intimidating simulation of his own house. The PA system roared again "It is not just the people that make a house into a home, the chores also have a part in it. So you have to do all the daily chores within the stipulated time and according to the instructions of your parents. Failing which you will be killed at the hand of their simulations." "Killed!? It's bad enough with these two creepy puppet like simulations meant to be my parents breathing down my neck, but death! That's a whole different story." Never in his life had Sam done any daily chores. More importantly, never in his life had both his parents been home to make him do the chores. As his mind was swimming in thoughts, he heard the bell ring which indicated that the round had started and a timer appeared before him with a time set for 10 hours. "10 hours!? Just how many of these chores are there?", he exclaimed. As the chores went by, his body kept getting more and more exhausted as it was carrying the damage from the previous tasks too. He was totally drained out. Sweat was dripping down his forehead and his face. His new clothes were totally drenched. Doing the dishes, laundry, cleaning all the rooms, dusting, cooking three meals, taking out the trash, making the bed , tidying the cupboards, buying groceries... so many chores and so little time. He had so much to do but not much time left. 4 hours...3hours...2hours... as he approached into the final hour, his body had given in. He just did not have it in him to vacuum the whole house and then lastly plunge the toilets. But, he put in every last ounce of energy left in his body to complete these chores and with 18 minutes still left on the clock, he lied down in submission. The system spoke up for one last time "Congratulations Player1, you have successfully completed our Mind Test Simulation. You will be blipped back into your world in 5...4...3...2...1..." A bright streak of light descended from above and suddenly he was in his room in the City all rejuvenated. His mind felt independent and free. Teenage problems, they were gone. As he had bent his mind to overcome his problems, he did not have to suffer from the dark side of teenage anymore. "Mind is a powerful weapon,I guess." He achieved all of this because of his own wit, grit and determination to be good at all that the adults stand against.... A GAME.

3

THE CALL OF JUSTICE

1993, a cold December evening. A 7 year old Chris was sitting at his window waiting for his parents to arrive from their business trip to DC. Both of them were job holders in the financial department of reputed corporates. He sat on the window for hours.... Waiting. Finally as the evening started to set in, he saw a black car pull up in their driveway. But it wasn't theirs. He went downstairs waiting for the door to open nonetheless. As door opened, two men wearing black clothes with a weary look on their faces proceeded towards him and asked, "Where are your grandparents, dear boy ?" "Grandpa's out back and grandma's in the kitchen I think." "Could u call them both to meet us out here please?" "Grandma, grandpa ! Somebody's asking for you at the front lawn.", called out Chris in the shrill voice of an elementary schooler. As his grandparents followed his call, they sensed something was wrong when they saw both the gentlemen looking at the grass with tear filled eyes. They instructed Chris to go upstairs to his room. He went inside but hid behind the kitchen door from where he could hear the whole conversation. As he heard them tell his grandparents that both his parents had died, he stood still in his boots. He couldn't move. He could only see . He saw as his grandparents burst into tears on hearing this. He saw them looking upto his room with a hand on their mouth. He saw them closing the door, sitting on the living room couch and crying their eyes out. By this time, he was in his room. He was too shocked to even let a tear out his eyes. What he had just heard had totally warped his mind. But, as he tried to wrap his head around this fact, he started sobbing inconsolably. He was back to the land of living but the world was more colourless than ever. His grandparents heard him crying and came up to check if everything was alright 'cause as per their knowledge, he didn't know anything about what had happened. As they entered his room, the first question he asked was "How did they die ?" Shocked at being confronted with this question, grandpa replied "Umm... They had uhh.. an accident." Apparently they were driving back and were passing a hilly region when a truck came and hit them dead on. "It was an instant and painless death", they said. "But it's painful for me. I don't even get to see the body. I don't get to say goodbye. It's seriously messed up." They left him to allow him time to tend to his own thoughts. The day of the funeral had come soon enough. Chris had not come out of his room even for his meals for the past few days. But he wasn't going to miss the funeral. This was the closest chance he could get of saying goodbye to his parents. So he got up, got ready and went downstairs with his eulogy in his hand. As the funeral was nearing its end, his turn came up to read out his eulogy. With teary eyes and a low voice, he read out his eulogy which ended with "In the end ashes to ashes and flames to flames. That's what life is." Although the funeral had ended, the case was still going on. Meanwhile his grandma was encouraging him to move on. She'd say "When you lose someone, there's a knot in your stomach that you think is gonna be there forever. But slowly with the passage of time, the knot starts coming untied and eventually you reach a phase when you realize that you haven't thought of that person the whole day and that's when you've actually moved on. But it's a difficult process and some days will surely be harder than the others. But, both of us are here to be with you and support you through it all and little by little you'll get there, poco a poco. " A few months went by with the case still being fought at the court. Finally it was verdict day. Not only did they get a measly compensation, but they lost the case too. Later that day, the defence lawyer came to their house and told his grandparents that the prosecutor was really incompetent. "I have a duty of care towards my clients so I have to do right by them. But there were clear and visible loopholes in the case which could make my client go to jail but the prosecutor failed to exploit them. I'm so sorry for your loss but at the end of the day the system is what it is." Hearing this, A shock wave of emotions went up his body. A mix of terror,anger,shock,grief,etc. and suddenly it felt like on the left there was nothing right and on the right there was nothing left. It was that day he decided to become a lawyer, to prevent what had happened to his family from being materialized again to haunt any other home. So he started working towards this goal of becoming a lawyer. From junior high itself he began to show great potential and unparalleled aptitude in the field of law. Be it the MUNs or Moot Court, he never forgot to leave his mark. There was a persuasive way he would present his cases that would force the judges and the delegates to spin their head in his direction with amazement. He passed junior high as valedictorian, while building his portfolio up the whole time. He was totally into social work and community service. He was also on the school football team. In high school he was the centre of attention. From "The kid who lost his parents", he got converted into "the popular kid with mysterious green eyes". He had become a hunk indeed. With a 6 feet 2 inch height, athletic build, bundles of lean muscle and 6 pack abs. His face was complete with a stark jawline, emerald green eyes, a dazzling smile , a fair complexion and his messy hair spread all over his forehead. He had become the kind of boy you would only read about in books. But staying all aloof from the potential in that sphere, he had his focus glued on becoming a lawyer. Needless to say, he totally rocked it on the academic front in high school, graduating as the salutatorian of his class. Given his fantastic profile, he could easily get into Harvard for a three year bachelors degree in English but instead he chose to be in a community college where the attendance wasn't an issue in order to attain a degree and at the same time prepare for LSAT and learn more about the American Law for the next three years. LSATs came... he totally aced them getting a 178. He was admitted into Harvard without having to break much of a sweat. He pursued the Juris Doctor course with all pomp and enthusiasm outperforming his classmates in moot courts and ethics class demonstrations. He passed out , second in his class of 1500 with a job application of one of the best law firms in the world, Price Waterhouse in his hands. From there on there was no looking back. He said he'd become a lawyer and so he did and so did he. As an associate he worked tirelessly with sleepless nights and cups of coffee as his only companions.

He didn't want to marry as he knew he would not be able to devote time for his domestic duties because he was so overpoweringly passionate about his professional ones. His hardworking nature was duly rewarded with constant promotions and timely increments. The number of hours he would bill in a month was totally crazy. But he could afford to put it all on his job as he had nothing to lose. Associate.... Special Associate.... Junior Partner..... Senior Partner...... and finally Managing Partner.. the post he had so wished and dreamt for all his life. But he couldn't consider himself a lawyer as long as he couldn't bring some semblance of justice towards the memory of his parents. He had a perfect record till date as in he had never lost a case he had touched and oh boy, did the people who were keen to break his record cross lines to achieve this. But they all bit the dust nonetheless. As part of their Corporate Social Responsibility obligations, the firm took on eight pro bono cases throughout the year as required by the law. In such cases, the firm charged zero fees from the client and represented the plaintiff,i.e. the ordinary citizen instead of the defendant, i.e. a body corporate. This was the last one for this year. A 43 year old man and his 39 year old wife had been hit by a raging car beside a gorge and their car fell off the deep end killing them both. The plaintiff was their 21 year old son and the defendant was a 47 year old white male, George Clifford. This case resonated with his childhood trauma too much that he just couldn't pawn it off to any other lawyer in the firm. He just had to fight it even though he knew this case was hitting a little too close to home and that he may experience painful emotions fuelled by his childhood baggage. "Finally a chance to do you justice, mom and dad.", he said, looking up to the heavens hoping they were up there. Next day the plaintiff came to his chambers so that Chris could prepare him for the deposition scheduled to be held for the day after. Chris prepared the client for the deposition and he could sense that it was a strong case. This lifted up his spirits. The deposition came. The defence totally teared apart the plaintiff. They made it look like it was the deceased's fault that both cars had collided and that the case should be dismissed on this ground alone. Only then did Chris realize what he was up against.The next day, the defence filed a motion to dismiss. Chris worked all night that day to present additional evidence so that the case doesn't get dismissed. He found a camera footage of the accused's son being drunk and presented it to the court. The defence argued that this was irrelevant but Chris asserted that it was relevant as in his statement he said that he was in the car with his dad the night of the accident so the father might have been distracted with helping out his son and hit the deceased's car. The judge found it worthy of a trial and tossed the motion to dismiss. Chris was kinda relieved to not be working in the gray area in this case and to not be looking for loopholes in laws and instead asserting and proving the application of those very laws. The next two weeks, he worked his back off to make the case affidavit and prepare his arguments. It was the day of the trial. Both the sides presented their opening arguments and both of them were pretty fantastic. The jury was amazed at how well both the sides of cases were being presented. Now it was time for the respective witnesses to take the stand. Chris ripped the defence witness off to shreds during cross questioning. But, the witness nonetheless committed perjury, which both the sides knew. It was time for the prosecution witness to take the stand. After the routine pledge, Chris questioned the witness to present his case but during the cross questioning the defence lawyer virtually slashed the witness' head off to the point of tears. Their witness was a mess but Chris did not lose hope. That was until the defence shamelessly fabricated evidence and presented it to the court. He argued that it was inadmissible but it was ruled that the evidence was admissible. "I have no choice left now but to appeal to the emotions of the jury." It was time for the closing arguments. The defence presented pretty convincing arguments and made it a herculean task for Chris to turn the jury in his direction. But he made an appeal to the jury's emotions. He told them his backstory and how he became a lawyer and why he became a lawyer and how this case resonates with his past life. He ended with "The system did not do my family justice but I hope it does not wreck another family by depriving them off the justice that they deserve be it in a positive or a negative way. Thank you for your time." The jury went into the private enclosure to discuss about the verdict. Meanwhile Chris was sweating like crazy. His heart was beating as fast as a cheetah and his head felt dizzy. The pressure and gravity of the case had finally gotten to him. As the jury came out of the room, Chris was shivering with fear of the verdict being in opposition to his interests and all his work to do justice to his parent's memory going down the drain. The jury read out its verdict, "The accused has been sentenced by the court to seven years in jail. You may report to Darwin Correction Centre within 24 hours or cut a plea deal and inform the jury of the same." Hearing this verdict, tears flowed down Chris' cheeks as rapidly as the Hudson River. He had finally done it . He now just wanted to go back to his office and sleep on his office couch. Not his home, his office. He wanted to sleep in the enclosure which enabled him to deliver justice. As he reached there, a young man in his early 20s was waiting for him. He told Chris the whole story. That it was him who was at the wheel and not his dad. His dad was only covering for him to protect his future. Hearing all this, Chris called the father immediately to his office and cut a plea deal wherein he dropped the criminal charges and pressed only civil charges keeping in mind the son's future. He dropped the prison term but added in a 10 million dollars worth of compensation for the plaintiff. The father accepted the plea deal and the father son-duo left the office teary-eyed. It was then that he finally felt completely whole. The knot in his stomach, it was finally gone. He went up to the roof of his office and caressing the cross on his neck, he looked up to the heavens and said, "Mom,Dad, I've finally done it !!"

4

THE INFINITE ROTATIONS

Brazil! Brazil! Ole! Ole! Ole! Brazil! Brazil! Ole! Ole! Ole! The stadium was jampacked. It was the 1974 world cup semifinal. Brazil vs Holland, a surely promising prospect. All the TVs were on in Sao Paulo. A 10 year old Alexio was watching his father Abrahan playing which could be in all likeliness his last international match. The match was going on pretty smoothly until Brazil conceded 2 goals at the eleventh hour and lost the match. The fans sure weren't happy. There was a lot of violence both in and outside the stadium. As the team flew into the country, they were subject to all types of objects being thrown at their team bus. Abrahan sure didn't exactly picture his international career ending this way. As he was coming out of the team bus, a fan out of nowhere ran towards him with a zombie-like aggression and hit both his knees dead on with a hockey stick. Abrahan immediately collapsed and was taken to the hospital where he was treated with knee replacement which meant an abrupt and untimely end to not just his international but his football career as a whole.

That day as he saw his father being brought into the ICU, he drilled it into his mind to become a successful footballer and ensure that the Diaz name is etched into the golden pages of history. “If it couldn’t be you Pai, It’s surely gonna be me.” Thus started the career of a legendary footballer who was about to let the world know the beauty of football. He would train and train hard. In the scorching tropical heat, he would not see time as a measure of his hardwork but the number of mugs of sweat he let off by squeezing his T-shirt during the training session. His hardwork paid off when he was selected onto his high school football team. It was the final of the Nascimento Youth League. Their school team was trailing by two in the first half of the game versus Kings International but Alexio scored three goals in the second half to successfully help his team win the title. It was then that he was finally noticed by his city folk. He got into college with a sports scholarship. In college, he would train everyday at a barren piece of abandoned land near a man made lake. One day, as he was training, a Santos FC scout was passing by and saw him train. His experienced eyes spotted trophies worth of potential in this young 19 year old boy. The scout gave Alexio his contact info and asked him to meet up at the club stadium next weekend. He did as he was asked to and rendezvous-ed with the scout at the club stadium. He introduced Alexio to the assistant coach. “This fine gentleman will be taking your trial”, said the scout pointing to a bulky gentleman on his left. He went with the assistant coach and put on a jersey. Alexio was asked to do a few drills before the team was divided into two teams for the purpose of a trial match with the aspirants on one side and the team players on the other. Alexio was totally the centre of attention with two goals and an assist. From there on there was no looking back. The next day a contract was signed with him which gave him entry to the legendary Santos FC and to follow in the wake of legends such as his father and Pele himself. He totally outshone all the players in the Division B league which the club ended up winning with Alexio getting the Golden Boot. That year, he also won the Rising Star Award conferred by FIFA to up and coming footballers. In no time he was making jokes in the shower with the players of the senior team. He was playing in the big leagues. Santos FC eventually ended up winning the Brazilian National Cup that year too. He was the apple of the eye for Brazilian football fans. The national selectors further decided to give him one more feather to add to his cap by selecting him to be on the national team for the upcoming 1986 Mexico Football World Cup. The national team ended up underperforming that year, bowing out in the quarters by losing in the penalty shootout to France. Once again Alexio was made to relive the memories from 1974 which he would rather forget. Meanwhile Santos FC was continuing its winning streak of winning the National Cup 5 times in a row. Alexio was a part of every subsequent Brazilian World Cup Squad. The squad ended up bowing out in the Round of 16 of the 1990 by losing with a one goal margin versus arch rivals Argentina. It was a dark period for Alexio. He was totally demotivated and didn't want to play anymore but in these dire times it was his father who motivated him and cheered him up and finally Brazil won the World Cup in 1994 with Alexio finally getting the Golden Boot. He gained recognition as the "Striking Phenom" all around the world. The Alexio Virus had taken over the world by storm. These were all the memories that Alexio was reminiscing as he sat in his hotel room enjoying a nostalgic evening before he played his last football match... The 2002 FIFA World Cup, South Korea and Japan final match with Germany at the International Stadium in Yokohama. This was his last chance of realizing his teenage dream and get the judgement after years of pleading his case. Will the date and the name and the match and everything else be recorded on a black or a golden page in the Brazilian football history book? Will it be a hall of fame or a hall of shame? It all depended on what the stars had in store for him tomorrow. But what is important right now is that he gets a good night's sleep in order to be at his top energy level in the high voltage game tomorrow. So he pressed the pillow below his head and escaped into the world of fancy. His dad was flying all the way over from Brazil to watch the game, a fact that provided him with as much pressure as motivation. The daylight was gleaming with a serene brightness at the heart of the Land of The Rising Sun as the players of both the teams were getting ready for a match that could make or break a team, the world cup final. 80000 fans, commentators of various countries going crazy in the media enclosure meanwhile fans chanting a slogan that they had composed for their very own Alexio- "Go,go Alexio ,we're with you! Striking Phenom,shooting venom,we're with you! " As Alexio made it out the players' tunnel and onto the pitch, the fans let out a great and loud cheer for him and started chanting the slogan with even more vigour and accompanied by a rhythmic clapping of hands. The atmosphere was truly magical. As the commentators described it "It is a game where the stakes couldn't be any higher. The world cup trophy. That's what both the teams here are fighting for. A great game of football can be conveniently expected from these two well oiled and experienced machines. But at the end of the day , the team that dominates the midfield will home the title for the coming four years, according to me."There was a growing uproar in the field as the kick off was over with and the ball was rolling freely on the ground. Brazil was playing with an immaculate passing strategy with an aim to retain maximum possession while Germany wanted to just concentrate on their defending and somehow manage to take the game to the penalty shootout where they would rely on their explosive shooting power. Their formations further made this clear as Germany was going with the classic 5-4-1 while Brazil was going with the slightly innovative 4-2-3-1 . Brazil was passing the ball around the box but to no avail. Germany's man marking was outstanding. But Brazil was playing a passive game. It was letting the opposition play a few passes in their own half and was only starting to press when the ball crossed the mid line. The first half was kinda boring for the fans with the ball just rolling from everywhere to everywhere but to no avail. Both the teams were yet to open the scoresheet. Brazil was attacking through the right wing this time. A wonderful and speedy counterattack, a crafty cross into the box to Alexio, he kicks the ball on the volley but an unreal save by the goalkeeper and the scores stay level. As the commentators described it, "God's great hand saves Germany from falling back in this high voltage Finale." The rest of the first half passed without anything eventful other than this attack happening. As both the teams receded into their dressing rooms, Alexio realized that he had to take charge. He had to motivate his teammates in order to take home the championship title that they so rightfully deserve. The coach instructed them to change their formation to the classic attacking 3-4-3 and to play totally physical and aggressive pressing football and specially told Alexio to use the indigenous Ginga style wherever and whenever possible as he was the only player in the team who held the mastery of this majestic game changing style. The second half commenced with both the sides changing halves. Brazil now had to attack from the left wing which now put even more responsibility on Alexio's shoulders. Brazil was now pressing and rushing towards the ball in a madman-like but organized way. Germany was totally taken aback by this sudden change of pace in the Brazilian game. But the downside of this move was that even though they had taken control over possession, the Brazilian side hadn't yet broken the deadlock and they were conceding a lot of fouls which awarded Germany free kicks from potentially dangerous positions. It was the 58th minute when a German player was anticipating a header but to prevent that from happening, Alexio put his boot up higher than to the referee's liking, who blessed Germany with a free kick at the edge of the penalty box while cursing the Brazilians with a yellow card to Alexio. The freekick was beautifully taken. It was swinging and curling to exactly the unguarded section of the net but thankfully was a little too high and as a result it met the crossbar and was deflected out of play. A fantastic goal kick from the Brazilian keeper and Brazil were back on the counter. The central midfielder made a beautifully precise pass to Alexio on the left wing who took the ball to the corner flag and intended to penetrate the defence from that position. A fantastic rainbow to beat the first defender and the Ginga was on. The spectators could finally see the real,unfiltered beauty of the game at the feet of Alexio. He defeated one defender, another,another and now faced only the last line of defence, the goalkeeper. He made the shot at the far post and the keeper made a screamer of a save. The whole German team was up in celebration. The keeper had still kept the game alive. The momentum of the game from there on increased dramatically. From an attack-defense game, it had become a box-to-box game. The fans were feeling the energy and so were the players. This is the type of a World Cup final that you'd expect to see from two teams of such humongous stature. It was the 65th minute. Brazil had crafted a witty attack from open play. The central midfielder took the ball right to the edge of the box and passed it onto the left winger who passed it onto the right wing. The right winger came into the box but back passed it to the striker who was a few metres away from the box. This move totally scrambled the defence, with the goalkeeper being the only one standing between striker,i.e., Alexio and the net. Alexio made a fiery shot and it went past the keeper and into the net. GOAL!!!! BRAZIL!!! Alexio had finally broken the deadlock at the 67th minute with a howler of a shot. "Probably the greatest goal of the tournament", the commentators said. Play resumed and Brazil, who had gained confidence from the opening goal now played with a royal charm, eager to score the security goal and it came soon enough. It was the 79th minute. Alexio was dangerously entering the box when an opposition defender put in an untimely tackle gifting Brazil a free kick from a favourable position. Alexio took a beautiful free kick and all the defender had to do was head the ball into the net. It was another goal and Brazil had more or less sealed their victory and a spot in the golden pages of football history. The celebrations were unparalleled in the stadium. The rest of the match went by without much happening and just like that Brazil was crowned the World Champion. Alexio had done it. He had done what his father could not. With a goal and an assist he was the named the Player Of The Match. He was also the recipient of Golden Boot for scoring a baffling 18 goals throughout the tournament. As the trophy came in, he called his father onto the pitch to come and lift the trophy along with the whole team and so Abrahan did. It was a picture worthy of the newspapers and magazines. Father and son lifting the trophy together in the wake of the rest of the team. In the midst of this numbing happiness, Alexio thought to himself, "I've finally done it Pai, Diaz name, golden page it is." A dream end to the career of a footballer who taught the whole world how to dream. A legend, a pioneer , a Striking Phenom indeed.

5

LA VOYAGE ALPHABETIQUE

"Nap....ol...eon... uhh.. forced..... Austria....to....sign....a....tr....." "A treaty, Matteo. How is it possible that this is your second year of middle school and you are still having difficulty in reading such simple words." "But, teacher, concentrating is so boring and tough, why to do it at all ?" As he said these words, the whole class burst out in laughter. The teacher too was lowkey smiling with her hand on her forehead. "Just sit down,Matteo." This is what Matteo was known for. He was the class clown. The person who could make you laugh in the dullest of situations and at his dumbest of jokes. But studying, nah-uh , definitely not his cup of tea. He was born and brought up till now in the Italian city of Milan. He was born eight months into his mother's pregnancy. So, the family expected complex complications. But instead, they got a fairly normal child apart from his disinterest in studying, which was the characteristic of one in every five students. He had a seemingly normal childhood. But the problem of reading, writing and comprehending was always there. The parents were reluctant to take him to a child psychologist for the fear of social stigma so they made him take IQ tests at home. In each of these tests, it was determined that he had an IQ well above the national average. So how come he couldn't perform well in tests ? That was the question that his parents have been pondering on for quite a while now. His parents were filthy rich. They had a hospitality business right here in Milan. Grimolini Premium Stays was his parents' hotel chain spread all over the country but centred at Milan. All their hotels were premium with a minimum 5 star rating. Their hotels were a thoroughfare for Italian celebrities from all kinds of spheres. Due to all this wealth, he did not even feel the need to study. He was set to inherit the country's most prestigious hotel chain. Where did grades figure into all this ? "You don't carry your grades to your grave, you know?", he'd say. But he had a knack for sports, especially football. In a country where football was the most popular sport and where every single match looked like a carnival both inside and outside a stadium, this was a great skill to improve on. He was a good player but not good enough to make it to the big leagues. So, no hope in that department too. The only place he felt away from any judgement was beside his friends. They were the craziest bunch of humans he had ever met with their pranks, weird games and whatnot. It was beside them that he really belonged. Matteo barely passed middle school. But by the time he was in high school, his Dad had his first heart attack at the age of 42. Thankfully a triple bypass surgery saved his life. This event further strayed his mind away from studying. Whenever confronted by his mom, he'd say "Mom, you see how short and uncertain life is ? Why do you want me to waste it on superficial things like tests and studies and homework ?" His Mom had no words. His utter disregard for his studies was driving her mad. But she dealt with the problem in the most cliché way possible. She ran away from the problem. She began to neglect Matteo, not that he cared. But in her defence, she had her hands full from taking care of her husband and managing the company in the interim period. Struggle and battle through life ? Nah... He was more of a live,love,laugh your way through life kinda guy. He had a strange affinity towards numbers. He literally has been acing arithmetic ever since he was a kid while failing miserably in all other subjects, even algebra. One day, a group of psychologists came to the school to evaluate students on certain parameters for the purpose of a sample survey required by the government to make certain amendments to some existing laws relating to education. Matteo was one of the students who was selected to be evaluated. The selection was done on a lottery or lucky draw basis so that the information presented by the sample survey is not biased at all. All the students were evaluated one by one. On asking around, the questions being asked were general ones usually used for the purpose of introductions. Apparently, the students were also being made to sign a consent form, giving their full consent to participate in this exercise. At last, it was Matteo's turn. He was lowkey excited to answer the questions asked by the psychologists. He went in, greeting the doctor with a dazzling smile and a formal greeting, "Bonjourno!" Before being asked the questions, he was given a consent form and was asked to fill that first. He started filling the form. The doctor noticed that Matteo was having abnormal difficulty in writing and was making pretty fundamental and basic spelling mistakes. Moreover, he was also frequently asking the read out version of simple words from the doctor. The doctor noticed all this but sat there patiently with a smile on his face, waiting for him to complete the formalities. After Matteo was done filling up the consent, the doctor pulled out a different questionnaire. It was a Harvard approved questionnaire to determine whether a student was dyslexic or not. He asked the questions and Matteo answered them with ease. The doctor let Matteo go without saying anything else. But, then he announced he was taking a short break . He went to the principal's office to discuss Matteo's condition in the presence of his teacher. Both the principal and the teacher were shocked to hear this. But they couldn't help but agree that everything made so much more sense now. "He's dyslexic", the doctor said. "Its not that he doesn't want to study or doesn't try to study. He wants to study and tries to be good at it too. But, it's just too hard for him. The conventional teaching methods are doing no good. He has to be taught using certified dyslexia-friendly teaching methods like mind maps." The next day Matteo along with his parents was called to meet the principal. "I haven't done anything wrong", Matteo replied to his parents' constant queries about any recent antics at school. His father was well and fine now and was back to business. Having the burden of management removed off the shoulder of his mother, she started devoting her time towards Matteo as any other parent should do. "He has dyslexia", the teacher pronounced much to the shock of Matteo and his parents "That can't be possible. I'm not dumb", Matteo asserted. But realizing the weird amount of sense this fact made in relation to Matteo's grades and his slow progress forced his mother to ask "So how can it be cured." "It is not a disease. It is a difficulty. So conventional teaching methods will not help him. He has to study using innovative techniques such as mind maps, flow charts, etc." His parents decided to let him come to school so that hc can at least attempt to understand the lessons and at the same time they hired a specialized home tutor who would make Matteo understand the concepts in a dyslexia-friendly way. All was going fine and his grades were also improving steadily until his father was convicted and had to serve a 10 year jail term for insider trading. He felt miserable of the fact that he did not even know there was a pending case being tried at court against his father. "Was it not your duty to tell me, Mom?" asked Matteo with tear filled eyes. "We did not want to bother you, honey. Moreover, I truly believed that your father was innocent as he claimed to be . It is only now that I am realizing that he was capable of something like this too " That day, Matteo spent the whole day crying his eyes out in his room feeling utterly betrayed by his own family. His Mom took charge as CEO of the company. Being the CEO meant going back to neglecting her son as per her parenting which was by no means a healthy parenting method. When Matteo realized that his mother was neglecting him at a time when he needed her the most, he felt as if somebody had pushed him off a cliff and he had fallen into a dark pit. He was totally out of control. Drinking excessively, taking drugs, excessive late night partying, missing his school and home lessons and shutting himself out from the rest of the world was not fairing him well. But where were his friends at this time? I guess nobody wants to be friends with a criminal's son. "Some friends they were !", Matteo exclaimed with disgust while he was high as a kite on weed. On instances where his Mom did notice his otherwise invisible existence, she'd say "Pathetic! Just look at what you're doing to yourself. Just look at yourself in the mirror. Is this a face you'd be proud to present? Whatever, you do whatever the hell you want. I have better things to do than to babysit your hopeless chassis." "Yeah, that's right Mom. Run away like you always do, like a fricking coward. The company's your baby now, not me. Some Mom you are.. huh ! ", exclaimed Matteo with contempt. He had fallen off the deep end with no one around him there to provide a hand in order to help him up. One day as he was going to the market, he met his principal. He could clearly sense something was gravely wrong with Matteo. He kept pestering Matteo to tell him what he had been doing the past few months. Finally giving in to annoyance, Matteo told him everything from A to Z. The principal took Matteo to a nearby park and gave him a strict talking-to. "What is wrong with you? The first sign of progress and you cut it off indefinitely. The parent issue is no excuse for you to fall off the rails. You want to be an adult so bad, start acting like an adult. Own up to your deeds and clean your own messes coz no one else is gonna do it for you. That's how it works in the real world. Your life is yours alone. If you don't try to shape it as per your specifications, you'll be inviting the world to shape it and trust me, the world is merciless. It will make you bleed out to death from a thousand paper cuts. Just think about what I just told you. Maybe some sense will magically prevail in that drug-filled brain of yours." The principal's words hit Matteo hard and shook him to the very core. He decided to get his life back on track and get his shit together. He admitted himself to a Substance Abuse Rehab Centre the next day. He thought he didn't have it in him to defeat his addiction but surprisingly he did. Months went by, 5 to be exact. He had not subjected himself to substance abuse for 5 whole months. From there on, his remission journey was easy. 2 months after, he came home from the centre and wanted to learn new things. That is when he heard about card tricks and sequences.He had always had an analytical mind and numbers had always fascinated him. He started watching youtube videos and started designing mind maps for himself so that he could understand the concept in the best possible manner. He devoted an awful amount of time to learning these tricks. After he thought he had mastered this art, he started going to casinos and getting into games. Poker mostly. He would figure out what cards the opponent has and play his hand accordingly. He was winning ridiculous amount of wealth. With the inflow of this easy money, came the will to leave his home and resettle. He left Milan and bought an apartment in Rome, the capital of Italy. He knew what he was doing illegal so he operated under the radar. He had a keen interest in the stock market and thus he needed this capital to invest in various companies. After a while, he quit this illegal hustle and started studying trading graphs. He would log on to the market 30 minutes after it opened and 30 minutes before it closed to analyse the tendencies and patterns of different companies when the market is at its most volatile state. While making all these analysis, he even created his own interpretations of stock performance graphs of different companies. He finally decided about the companies he wanted to invest in. After his father's imprisonment, his parents' company opened 50.08 % equity to the general public. Matteo utilized 90 percent of his funds to buy this 50.08% equity , which earned him a spot on the Board and also made him the single majority shareholder of the company. He utilized the rest of the funds to buy marginal equities in other companies that were doing well. Now that he was the majority stakeholder in his parents' company, he had to actively take part in decision and policy making. So he started analysing the hospitality market condition, consumer analysis in that department, stock and internal management analysis, productivity and profitability analysis,etc. Analysis , analysis .... This had become his life. Analysis from day in to day out. Matteo attended the Board meetings of his parents' company via video conferencing from Rome itself not feeling the need to go to Milan. His mother was absent in all of those meetings as she was apparently busy in foreign sales promotion campaigns, as the company was about to go international as per the model proposed by Matteo himself. He was making huge gains from all his investments. Year by year, his net worth was spiking up like crazy. He now established his very own Investment Banking firm and expanded his influence to related fields like crypto, drophipping,NFTs,etc. After seven years on the grind, he was finally pronounced the most successful trader in the history of trading. But, the late nights, the mind maps and the analysis tables and charts did not stop. He had totally cut ties from his parents. "If they could not bear to see me at my worst and tend to me then, they have no right to see me at my best and take advantage of my public image and goodwill now", he'd say. One day, as he was at the chemist's, he bumped into his principal. "Long time no see, old man" "That's still principal to you, boy" "Well okay, Mr. retired principal", replied Matteo laughing. They talked about the old times and how things have changed. "You've come a long way Matteo. I'm really proud of everything you have achieved." His eyes shone at hearing these words and his soul no longer had a hole. It was filled by the fulfilment of the desire to hear these words from someone whom he considered his father figure and his mentor. Matteo thanked him, took his blessings and headed home. He was feeling complete. He was having his "I've made it" moment . Who would've thought that a dyslexic like himself would be the subject of numerous articles and magazine covers. “That’s all it takes. A little hardwork, to join the Hall of Fame of any field you desire to choose in life. Look at me , from writing deformed alphabets in my notebook to writing perfect alphabets on my employees’ paychecks, I’ve come a long way. Grit, determination with a mix of hardwork.... That’s all it took for a dyslexic to become a world- renowned hustler.”, that’s all he had to say to conclude the speech he was invited to deliver by the principal at his old high school.

Printed by Libri Plureos GmbH in Hamburg,
Germany